Whales and Dolphins

Our Friends in the Sea

Barbara Todd

SCHOLASTIC

AUCKLAND SYDNEY NEW YORK LONDON TORONTO
MEXICO CITY NEW DELHI HONG KONG

This book is dedicated to
all our "friends in the sea"

First published 1999
Scholastic New Zealand Limited
Private Bag 94407, Greenmount, Auckland 1730, New Zealand.

Scholastic Australia Pty Limited
PO Box 579, Gosford, NSW 2250, Australia.

Scholastic Inc
555 Broadway, New York, NY 10012-3999, USA.

Scholastic Limited
1-19 New Oxford Street, London, WC1A 1NU, England.

Scholastic Canada Limited
123 Newkirk Road, Richmond Hill, Ontario L4C 3G5, Canada.

Scholastic Mexico
Bretana 99, Col. Zacahuitzco, 03550 Mexico D.F., Mexico.

Scholastic India Pte Limited
29 Udyog Vihar, Phase-1, Gurgaon-122 016, Hayana, India.

Scholastic Hong Kong
Room 601-2, Tung Shung Hing Commercial Centre,
20-22 Granville Road, Kowloon, Hong Kong.

© Barbara Todd, 1999
All photographs by the author with the following exceptions:
Blue whale (page 8-9) Mark Carwardine
Humpback whale (page 10) David Fleetham
Sperm whale (page 13) Mark Jones

ISBN 1-86943-392-0

9 8 7 6 5 4 3 2   0 1 2 3 / 0

Illustrations by Richard Gunther
Typeset in Tiepolo Book 16/20 pt
Printed by SRM Productions Services, Malaysia

Contents

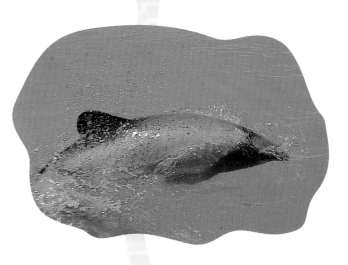

Did you know . . .   5

Whales and Dolphins   10

Mammals   14

Breathing   16

Flippers, Tailflukes and Dorsal Fins   18

Teeth and Baleen   20

Pods   22

Migration   23

Action   24

Identification   30

Whales, Dolphins and People   33

Index & Glossary   35

Did you know . . .

the biggest creature that has ever lived on this earth is a whale.

It's bigger than the biggest dinosaur.

Its heart is almost as big as a Volkswagon "beetle" car.

An elephant can stand inside its mouth.

Its baby is as big as a truck.

I wonder what kind of whale it is.

The biggest creature is a blue whale.

Some blue whales are 30 metres long . . .
That's about as long as 75 kids standing in a row.

An adult blue whale can hold 10 people on its flipper.

A baby blue whale gains 90 kilograms every day.
That's about as heavy as a grown man.

Whales and Dolphins

There are about 80 different kinds of whales and dolphins, and here are some of them.

This bottlenose dolphin is checking out the view above the water

Humpback Whale

A humpback mother and her new calf explore their underwater world

Dusky Dolphin

Pilot Whale

This pilot whale calf is only a few hours old. It will stay
close to its mother's side for many days

*Dusky dolphins love to play
and leap out of the water*

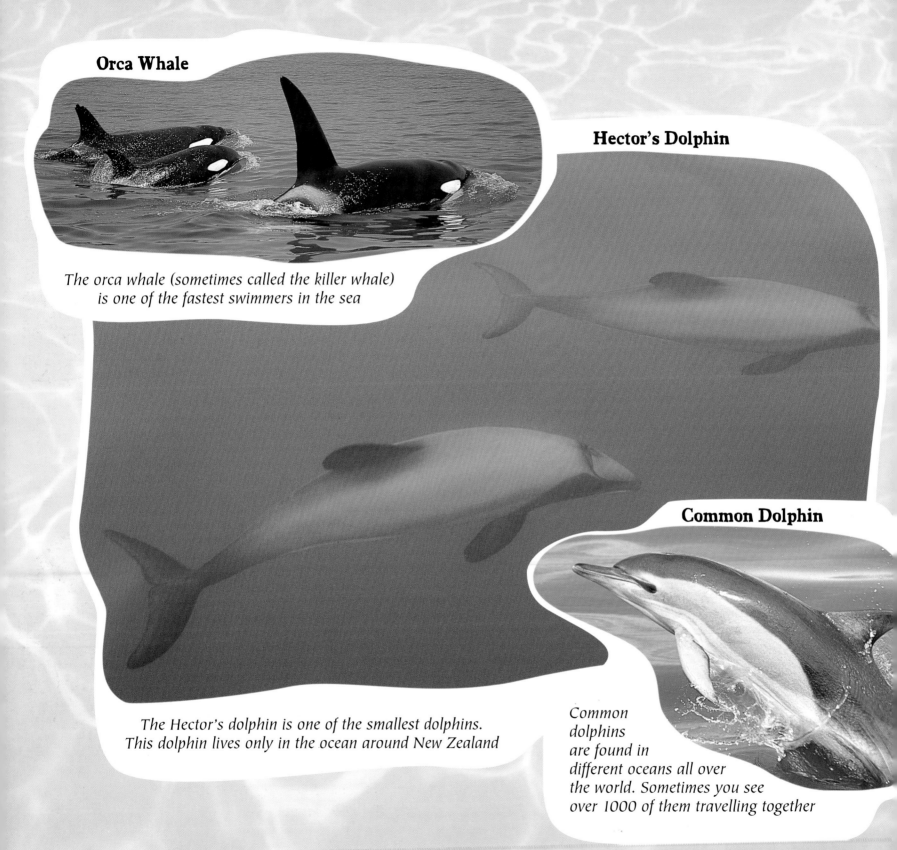

Orca Whale

The orca whale (sometimes called the killer whale) is one of the fastest swimmers in the sea

Hector's Dolphin

The Hector's dolphin is one of the smallest dolphins. This dolphin lives only in the ocean around New Zealand

Common Dolphin

Common dolphins are found in different oceans all over the world. Sometimes you see over 1000 of them travelling together

Right Whale

Right whales have patches of rough hard skin all over their heads. These patches, often white, are called callosities (kuh-_lohs_-uh-teez)

Southern Right Whale Dolphin

These southern right whale dolphins are real speedsters. They can swim almost as fast as orca whales

You could park 8 kids' bikes on a sperm whale's head.

Sperm Whale

The sperm whale has one of the biggest heads and the largest brain of any whale

Mammals

You might think whales and dolphins are big fish, but they're not. They're mammals — just like you.

Whale and dolphin young are called calves. The calves grow inside their mothers and are born alive — just like you.

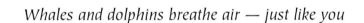

Whales and dolphins breathe air — just like you

This calf was born underwater and has come to the surface quickly to take a breath of air

Whale and dolphin calves drink their mother's milk and live with her until they can take care of themselves.

This newborn Hector's dolphin calf will stay with its mother for at least one year

Sometimes another 'auntie' whale or dolphin helps the mother take care of her new calf

Breathing

A whale's and dolphin's nose is on top of its head, and is called a blowhole. The blowhole opens when the whale or dolphin comes up to breathe, and closes very tightly when it dives underwater.

This whale's warm breath has formed water droplets in the cool air above the water

This dolphin's blowhole opened as soon as its head came out of the water

Imagine if your nose was on top of your head ...

This dolphin's blowhole is closed so no water can get inside

16

A whale's and dolphin's breath is called a blow, or spout.

Most dolphins have small blows or spouts

A blue whale's blow is 9 metres high.

Most whales have very high blows or spouts

17

Flippers, Tailflukes and Dorsal Fins

Instead of hands, whales and dolphins have flippers to help them steer and turn.

This bottlenose dolphin is using its flippers to help turn its body around in the water

Humpback whales have the longest flippers

Instead of feet, whales and dolphins have tailflukes. They swim by moving their tailflukes up and down.

A dusky dolphin uses its tailflukes to move through the water

Almost all whales and dolphins have dorsal fins on their backs.

Most dolphins have pointed fins

Hector's dolphins have round fins like Mickey Mouse ears

These southern right whale dolphins are different and don't have fins at all

A male orca's dorsal fin is about as tall as an adult human.

Male orca have the tallest fins — up to 1.8 metres

19

Teeth and Baleen

Most whales and dolphins have teeth. Toothed whales and dolphins usually eat fish and squid.

Squid

Some types of dolphins have over 200 teeth

Squid might look pretty weird, but whales think they taste great.

Dolphins use their teeth to grab their food and usually swallow it whole

Some whales have baleen instead of teeth. The baleen hangs from the top of the whale's mouth and has fringed, hairy edges. Baleen whales have hundreds of pieces of baleen in their mouths. Tiny fish or small sea animals called krill become trapped in the hairy edges of the baleen.

These krill will soon become the baleen whale's dinner

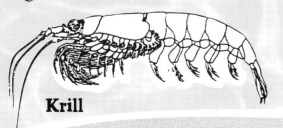

Krill

This humpback whale has a mouthful of water and krill. After it spits out the water, it will lick the krill off its baleen and swallow them

Pods

Whales and dolphins live in family groups called pods.

A small pod of orca

A large pod of spinner dolphins

Migration

Every year some whales go on a long journey called a migration. In winter they travel to warm waters to have their calves. In the summer they travel to cooler waters where they can find more food.

"I wonder if they've ever thought about whale road maps."

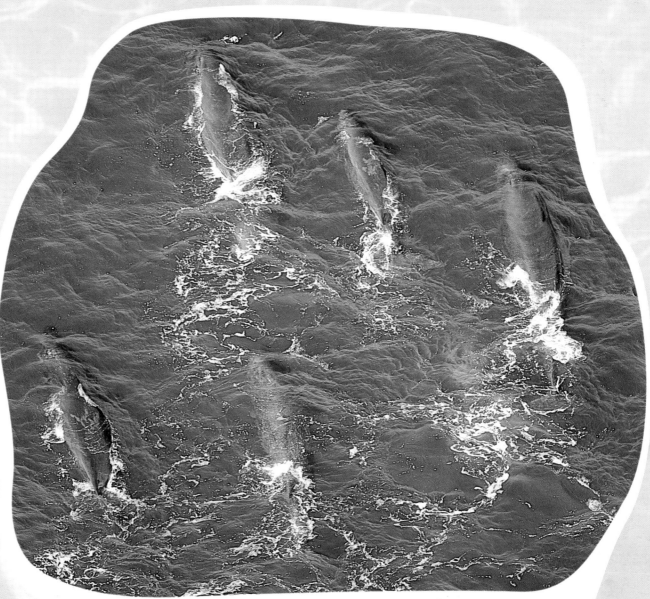

These sperm whales are migrating to cooler waters where they'll find lots of squid, one of their favourite foods

Action

When a whale or dolphin brings its head out of the water to look around, it is called spyhopping. When it brings its whole body out of the water, it is called breaching.

This orca is spyhopping. What could it be looking at?

This breaching humpback will make a big splash when its body hits the water

This breaching orca has brought almost all of its body out of the water

Some types of whales bring their tails up in the air before diving underwater.

A sperm whale dives down into the sea to look for its dinner

When they bang their tails on the surface of the water, this is called lobtailing.

When whales lobtail, their tailflukes make a loud noise as they hit the water

Sometimes whales lobtail to let other whales know where they are

Sometimes whales and dolphins just like to have fun.

These dolphins look like they're having a race

I can jump higher than you!

Some people call dusky dolphins the acrobats of the sea.

27

Now I'm upside down!

Whales and dolphins can do some pretty amazing things.

Leapfrogging dusky dolphins

28

As high as the birds . . .

and almost higher than the mountains

Identification

People who study whales and dolphins are called researchers. Sometimes they give the animals names that match the way they look.

This humpback's tailflukes are almost all white, so researchers call it Snow

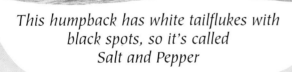

This humpback has white tailflukes with black spots, so it's called Salt and Pepper

This humpback's tailflukes are mostly black with patches of white and lots of spiky points. What would be a good name for it?

Sometimes researchers identify orca whales by looking at their dorsal fins.

These researchers are taking a photo of the orca's dorsal fin

Corkscrew is a male orca with a very crooked dorsal fin

Nicky is a female orca with a small nick in her dorsal fin

This male orca has two notches out of its dorsal fin. What would be a good name for him?

Right whales' callosities form patterns on their heads.

This right whale, with lots of callosities, likes to charge all over the ocean, so researchers call it Freight Train

This right whale likes boats and swims close by them looking "cool", so researchers call him Mr Cool

This callosity looks like a big nose. What would be a good name for the whale?

Whales, Dolphins and People

If you want to watch whales and dolphins and learn more about them, you can take a trip on a special whale- or dolphin-watch boat.

These dolphins are bowriding. They look like they're trying to race the boat

A dusky dolphin does a special leap to say hello

These people are watching a huge sperm whale dive into the sea

Maybe one day you'll get the chance to meet some whales and dolphins in their ocean home. They're very special and lots of fun.

Glossary

baleen — hangs from the upper jaw of baleen whales; has hairy ends

blow (spout) — whale's warm breath that forms a visible cloud of moist, misty air

blowhole — whale's nostril(s), located on top of its head

bowride — to swim in or ride the pressure wave in front of a boat

breach — to leap headfirst out of the water and land with a splash

callosities — hard growths of skin (somewhat like warts) on the heads of all right whales

dorsal fin — fin located on the backs of most whales and dolphins

flippers — front limbs of whales and dolphins

krill — tiny shrimp-like animals eaten by most baleen whales

lobtail — to slap the tailflukes on the water making a loud noise

migration — a regular journey between one area and another

pod — a group of whales or dolphins

spyhop — to raise the head out of the water and look around

squid — the food of many toothed whales and dolphins

tailflukes — whale's or dolphin's tail

Index

baleen 20
blow 17
blowhole 16
bowriding 33
breaching 24
breathing 14, 16, 17
callosities 13, 32
dolphins
__bottlenose 10, 18
__common 12
__dusky 11, 18, 27, 28, 33
__Hector's 12, 15, 19
__southern right whale 13, 19
__spinner 22
dorsal fins 18, 19, 31

fish 20
flippers 18
identification 30-32
krill 21
leapfrogging 28
lobtailing 25
mammals 14
migration 23
milk 15
pods 22
size (comparisons) 6-9, 13, 17, 19
squid 20
spout 17
spyhopping 10. 24
tailflukes 18, 25, 30

teeth 20
whales
__blue 8
__humpback 10, 18, 21, 24, 30
__killer 12
__orca 12, 13, 19, 22, 24, 31
__pilot 11
__right 13, 32
__sperm 13, 23, 25, 33

Note: Page numbers in italics refer to illustrations.

In 1980 Barbara Todd worked on a marine research vessel studying humpback whales in the Caribbean. When a fellow crew member became seasick she was happy to turn her six-week job into a four-month adventure — the beginning of a lifelong fascination with whales.

In 1983 she came to New Zealand from the United States to study sperm whales off Kaikoura on the east coast of the South Island. Five years later she teamed up with fisherman Roger Sutherland and the couple started New Zealand's first whale watching business in Kaikoura. In trying to explain the inexplicable — the mysterious emotional response that humans have for whales and dolphins — Barbara has decided that we may just be longing for a simplicity that has escaped us.

"For a brief moment while we are meeting whales
and dolphins, we can forget bank balances,
relationships and jobs, and become children again."

BARBARA TODD